Samuel French Acting

M000158894

Blacktop Sky

by Christina Anderson

SAMUELFRENCH.COM   SAMUELFRENCH.CO.UK

FOR PRODUCTION ENQUIRIES

UNITED STATES AND CANADA
Info@SamuelFrench.com
1-866-598-8449

UNITED KINGDOM AND EUROPE
Plays@SamuelFrench.co.uk
020-7255-4302

Each title is subject to availability from Samuel French, depending upon country of performance. Please be aware that BLACKTOP SKY may not be licensed by Samuel French in your territory. Professional and amateur producers should contact the nearest Samuel French office or licensing partner to verify availability.

MUSIC USE NOTE

Licensees are solely responsible for obtaining formal written permission from copyright owners to use copyrighted music in the performance of this play and are strongly cautioned to do so. If no such permission is obtained by the licensee, then the licensee must use only original music that the licensee owns and controls. Licensees are solely responsible and liable for all music clearances and shall indemnify the copyright owners of the play(s) and their licensing agent, Samuel French, against any costs, expenses, losses and liabilities arising from the use of music by licensees. Please contact the appropriate music licensing authority in your territory for the rights to any incidental music.

IMPORTANT BILLING AND CREDIT REQUIREMENTS

If you have obtained performance rights to this title, please refer to your licensing agreement for important billing and credit requirements.

BLACKTOP SKY had its world premiere produced by the Unicorn Theatre in Kansas City, Missouri (Cynthia Levin, Producing Artistic Director) on January 26, 2013. It was part of the A.C.T. First Look Series in January 2012, and was workshopped at the Providence Black Rep in 2009. The 2013 production was directed by Mykel Hill, with scenic design by Gary Mosby, costumes by Georgianna Londré Buchanan, lighting design by Alex Perry, assistant lighting design by Emily Swenson, and sound design by Dan Warneke. The Stage Manager was Tanya Brown. The cast was as follows:

IDA . . . . Chioma Anyanwu
KLASS . . . . Tosin Morohunfola
WYNN . . . . Frank Oakley III

PRODUCTION HISTORY

Know Theatre (OH): January 29, 2016 – February 20, 2016
Talawa Theatre Company (UK): June 11 – 27, 2014
Lower Ossington Theatre (CA): October 6 – 16, 2017
Theatre Seven of Chicago (IL): February 15, 2013 – April 21, 2013
Unicorn Theatre (MO): January 23, 2013 – February 2, 2013

CHARACTERS

IDA – Eighteen; Black American young woman. A realist, but also a romantic. Charming. Tough. Sweet.

KLASS – Twenty-five; Black American young man. A wanderer. Observant. Quiet. Poetic. Strong.

Jacket found

WYNN – Twenty-seven; Black American young man. Traditional. He prides himself on being a strong, sensible Black man. Plays tough, although he's rather sensitive.

THICK NECKS – Heard, not seen.

SETTING

Unnamed urban city; the blacktop courtyard of a housing project

Baltimore?

TIME

2008

AUTHOR'S NOTES

The =.= symbol represents unspoken moments filled with energy. It can be a moment when someone decides to do something (or not)/speak (or not speak). Or simply an active moment of looking, acknowledging.

When a "//" appears in a line of dialogue, the following line should begin:

IDA. You don't have to shout // about it.
WYNN. I'm not shouting.

REGARDING SOUND:
Neighborhood sounds function as a constant hum throughout the play. The sounds should explore the question(s): What does "class" sound like? What does the "ghetto" sound like?

The aural landscape should start out with "familiar" (some would say "stereotypical") notions of the projects or the ghetto. But slowly other sounds could trickle into the play. This shift could start when Ida and Klass look up at the sky for the first time. By the end of the play, it'd be great if the sounds are a collage of "upper" class sounds or "suburban" sounds, but are still considered a part of the "projects." If this doesn't make sense, feel free to ask the playwright for more details.

REGARDING KLASS' "STUFF":

Over the course of the play, Klass transforms the courtyard into his home. Each object he brings into the space has a specific and purposeful place. Even if its position doesn't make sense to us, it should be clear for Klass. He claims the entire playing space. Each object has a sense of beauty. The things he collects are definitely used and most likely broken, but beautiful nonetheless. When it all goes away, the emptiness should be palpable.

REGARDING TRANSITIONS:

Embrace them. Love them. Each one acknowledges and captures the passage of time. It's important for the lights, sound, and backstage crew to discover an artistic gesture that can usher us from one scene to the next. At their best, the transitions can create a moving portrait.

(Four buildings face each other to form the David L. Hynn [sounds like "hen"] Housing Projects. In the center there's a blacktop courtyard. And in the center of that courtyard are two busted, broken-down, rusted-up benches. Streaks of sunlight make their way around the looming apartment buildings.)

(We hear neighborhood sounds: children playing, men hollering, car horns, trucks, hip-hop music [with moments of reggae] plays from cheap radios or booming subwoofers. These sounds arrive in the courtyard as an echo, creating a world that is familiar yet distant.)*

(The sun sets on the benches.)

(Night stands up. Streetlamps turn on, casting a faint light across the courtyard.)

(The neighborhood sounds shift in mood to match the darkness of night, the arrival of artificial light.)

---

*A license to produce *Blacktop Sky* does not include a performance license for any copyrighted songs. The publisher and author suggest that the licensee contact ASCAP or BMI to ascertain the music publisher of any song they would like to use here and contact such music publisher to license or acquire permission for performance of the song. If a license or permission is unattainable for the song, or the licensee does not wish to use a song under copyright, the licensee may create an original composition or use a song in the public domain. For further information, please see Music Use Note on page 3.

Day

> (**IDA**, *perched on one of the benches, is in the middle of telling a story to a group of people who are unseen by the audience.*)
>
> (*She uses both benches as a stage, taking on the physical gestures of all the people who appear in her story. In another life, she would've been a great clown.*)

IDA. ...mindin' his own business.

He was standin' up there on Park and Ives, mindin' his own business.

He had this pocket radio that he kept close to his ear.

He was holdin' it up like this, (*Cups her hand against her left ear.*) like he's holdin' on to a lil bird.

And that bird is singin' some kind of sweet song.

A song he's tryin' to keep all to himself.

Antonio was straight up mindin' his own business.

He's standin' like this:

> (**IDA** *takes on Antonio's position. She holds the radio up to her ear, bops her head to a silent beat, scopes out the area around her.*)
>
> (*Snaps out of it:*)

And you know how he always has his stuff situated on the ground?

He has his display laid out all nice.

First he sweeps the sidewalk, then he takes that bright green sheet with the creamy white circles and folds it into a long rectangle.

He puts that on the sidewalk and on top of that he has all his merchandise:

the black leather wallets are there;

> (*Points out the location on the ground.*)

glass diamond necklaces here, painted gold rings there;

(Points it out.)

fake Coaches, Guccis, and Louis all set in its place, you know?

So Antonio's doin' his own thing.

The brotha had set up shop, waitin' for downtown tourists to come snatch up uptown product.

I was across the street, stepping out of check cashing.

Next thing I know I see these two cops talking to Antonio. Thick Neck dudes sorta got him cornered.

He's here *(Maps it out.)*

and the Thick Necks are here *(Maps it.)* and here. *(Maps it.)*

Thick Necks are standing like this:

> (**IDA** *takes on a wide stance. She hitches her thumbs in the waist of her pants.*)

First things first, Antonio holds up his radio like he's sayin', "It ain't a gun.

Don't get no trigger-happy ideas."

And he dangles it from the strap. A Thick Neck snatches it from him.

The other one says something to Antonio who says something back.

I can't hear what they talking about. I'm across the street. Can't hear anything over the traffic, the yelling, the music, the construction. It's so loud over there. Like it is over here. Like it is everywhere.

But I can see everything.

Every move, every twitch.

And Antonio's face is stone cold. That dude is keeping locked down.

Other people had stopped to watch – kids and old folks – but most everybody keeps walking, taking it in as they go by.

One of the Thick Necks turns to Antonio's merchandise, kneels down *(She kneels.)* and starts picking through it.

Antonio moves, looking like he's gonna stop him and I feel this chill go through me. It's like a thin slice of heat traveling from my heels up through me to my eyelids. The other Thick Neck blocks him.

(*Returns to her wide stance, blocks Antonio.*)

Then there's talking.

More talking.

Kneeling cop is picking at the necklaces, unzipping handbags.

Antonio's looking like that cop is diggin' into him, tossing him around.

Then over the noise, over the people, all over everything I hear Antonio yell:

"I DIDN'T DO NOTHIN'!"

And the block stops.

=.=

=.=

=.=

Freeze frame.

Red light.

Hold.

=.=

=.=

Kneeling cop is up on his feet.

Talking.

Talking.

Talking.

And then another police car pulls up.

Antonio's here. (*Maps it.*)

Four Thick Necks are here, here, here and here. (*Maps it.*)

Talking. Talking.

Another car.

Six Thick Necks: three here, (*Maps it.*) three here. (*Maps it.*)

A motorcycle.

Seven.

Talking. Talking. Talking.

Antonio is stone cold, his lips barely moving.

Then two of them Thick Necks just start shoving everything on the sheet towards the center.

Roughing up all of Antonio's stuff.

> (**KLASS** *enters, carrying a plastic crate packed full of metal objects, plastic cups, etc. He's wearing a winter coat with the hood up. It's lined with fake fur. He stands, listening to* **IDA***'s story.*)

Now you know Antonio don't handle his stuff like that.

His shit is organized like a street hustle.

He sees them treat his product like junk and he yells, "THAT'S MY PROPERTY! YOU CAN'T DO THAT TO MY STUFF!"

Thick Necks get agitated.

They move around him, acting like he's crazy, easily excited.

Hands up like, "Hey now, come on, no need for yelling." That kind of attitude.

A Thick Neck gathers the four corners of the sheet and scoops up everything.

Antonio's way of making money, surviving is choked up in this cop's hands.

Then Antonio just flips out.

He jumps towards his stuff.

A Thick Neck pulls out this taser, this yellow thing shaped like a gun, aims it at Antonio and then:

> (**IDA** *makes a long zapping sound, her hands tremble.*)

Antonio snaps back like he got plugged into a socket.

> (**IDA** *stands up on her toes, like someone or something has her by the back of the neck. She twists her face in pain. She yells.*)

> (**KLASS**, *startled, drops his crate. The crash seems to trigger* **IDA** *into the following series of movements: She folds her arms in front of her chest. Eyes roll back. She leans forward as if falling, but she catches herself. She leaps off the bench, stands on the ground. She snaps out of her trance.*)

But he ends up on the ground, rocking side to side.
Holding his chest.
Two Thick Necks manage to put him in handcuffs.
The back of my legs feel like they on fire.
I look down, makin' sure I'm alright.
The cop who zapped Antonio slips it back in its holder.
=.=

=.=

I wanted to do something, but I just walked away.
Came back here. Home.

> (**IDA** *looks over at* **KLASS**.)
>
> (**KLASS** *looks at her.*)
>
> (*He sits on one of the benches. He takes a can of grape soda from his pocket. He pops the top. Drinks.*)

Night

(Hours later.)

*(**KLASS** sits in the same spot. Asleep.)*

(His crate is tucked under his feet.)

(A streetlamp casts its artificial light across the blacktop.)

(A slim beam of light comes from offstage.)

*(**WYNN** enters behind a small flashlight connected to his keychain. **IDA** follows.)*

(They stop at the edge.)

IDA. *(Hushed.)* There. That was the last place I remember having 'em.

I was standing there telling everybody about Antonio.

> *(**WYNN** aims the light at the shape of **KLASS**.)*
>
> *(He clicks it off.)*

WYNN. *(Hushed.)* Uh-uh.

I am not going over there.

IDA. *(Hushed.)* What? Why? You scared?

WYNN. You want me to rough up some homeless dude in the middle of the night?

IDA. Wynn, my mama is gonna kill me if she finds out I lost another set of keys.

WYNN. Shouldn'ta been over there anyway.

IDA. You promised to help me.

WYNN. And I did, Ida.

We went all over, everywhere, retracing your steps.

And I'm standing here now realizing two things:

I'd do almost anything for you, but I'm not digging around that dude for your keys,

and two: maybe if you kept your behind at home, you wouldn'ta lost 'em in the first place.

IDA. Why don't you cut the bullshit talk and just pull out the damn leash, Wynn?

WYNN. It's not bull– leash? Leash? Ida, so now you sayin'
 I'm treating you like a dog?

IDA. Yeah, that's what I'm sayin', Wynn.

But you know what? You won't have to worry about
 me bein' out anywhere after my mama finds out 'cause
 she's gonna bust my ass up!

> (**KLASS** *shifts in his sleep.*)

> (**IDA** *and* **WYNN** *fall into the shadows. Hold
> their breath.*)

> (**KLASS** *settles into a comfortable position,
> continues his slumber.*)

=.= *(Waiting.)*

WYNN. =.= *(Waiting.)*

IDA. *(Hushed, whiny.)* Wyyyynn –

WYNN. Ida, no.

He's crazy.

Outta his damn mind.

Wearing a winter coat in June.

Lookin' like a fat pigeon.

I go over there talking 'bout, "My girl lost her keys."

He'd talk some crazy and then we'd have to throw down.

You want that?

IDA. I want my keys.

WYNN. Are you sure you lost 'em here?

Let's keep going over your steps.

If we still don't find 'em, we'll come back here.

Maybe he'll be gone by then...

IDA. I have a picture of me and you attached to one of the
 rings.

Somebody find my keys and know me...

they'd know where I live,

break in the apartment and steal all my stuff, Wynn.

WYNN. As many sets of keys you lost,

folks would've robbed your house five times over.

Everybody in the David L. Hynn towers knows Ida
Peters loses things all the damn time.

IDA. Are you finished?

WYNN. Yes.

IDA. Thank you.

Now stop being a punk,
and look for my keys.

WYNN. Who you callin' a punk?

IDA. The dude named Wynn,

who's too scared to walk around a damn bench
and look for my keys.

WYNN. =.=

IDA. =.=

> (**WYNN** *clicks on his flashlight.*)
>
> (*He crosses over to the benches, Black-secret-agent-style.*)
>
> (**KLASS** *sleeps.*)
>
> (**WYNN** *shines the light all around the empty bench.*)
>
> (*Nothing.*)
>
> (*He inches closer to* **KLASS**.)
>
> (*Closer. Closer.*)
>
> (*Shines the light around the occupied seat.*)
>
> (*Nothing.*)
>
> (*And then the light falls on* **KLASS**' *wrist.*)
>
> (*Ida's keys, the plastic frame holding a picture of Wynn and Ida, flash in the light.*)

WYNN. =.= (*A moment where the situation registers.*)

> (**WYNN** *calmly clicks off the light.*)
>
> (*Crosses over to* **IDA**.)

(*Slight, but surprising, hysteria.*) That crazy fuckin'
Pigeon taped the keys to his damn wrist!

IDA. What?

Awwww, my mama's gonna break my neck!

Lose my keys and then they end up with crazy Pigeon Man.

Wynn, you gotta get 'em.

WYNN. Fuck that!

IDA. What am I supposed to do then?

WYNN. Call the police.

IDA. I'm not calling the police.

WYNN. Why?

IDA. Police come around here

they'd zap him like they did Antonio.

I don't wanna be responsible for that shit.

He didn't steal 'em.

He found 'em.

WYNN. They have a better chance of getting 'em back than I would –

IDA. No cops.

=.=

I gotta figure out a place to sleep tonight.

WYNN. Come home with me.

IDA. I'm not goin' to your apartment with you.

WYNN. Why not?

IDA. Don't try and twist this into a tap session.

WYNN. *(Feigned shock.)* Ida!

IDA. Wynn this is serious.

WYNN. And I'm seriously and for real offerin' my baby some shelter.

Stay with me tonight.

We'll come back over here after I get off work and talk to him before the sun goes down.

Try to reason with him during the day.

Alright?

> (**WYNN** *grabs* **IDA**. *She resists at first but releases.)*

> (WYNN *kisses her lightly on the lips. She kisses him.*)

Tell your mama you're staying at your friend's house.

IDA. She don't like hearing things last minute.

Pisses her off.

WYNN. Ida you grown now.

Eighteen.

A high school graduate.

Got the diploma two weeks ago as proof.

You can stay over whoever's house you want to.

And I'm inviting you to rest against me until the sun comes up.

I can kiss you 'til you fall asleep; kiss those lips (*Re: down south.*) 'til you wake up.

> (*A smile slides across* IDA*'s face.*)

IDA. Okay. Alright. Let's go.

> (*She takes his hand. They cross in front of* KLASS *on the bench. They exit.*)

> (KLASS *opens his eyes, raises his head, and looks in the direction they walked.*)

> (*He was awake the entire time.*)

Sun Rises

(*Neighborhood sounds confront the sun.*)

(**KLASS** *remains on the bench.*)

(*He's asleep for real this time.*)

(**IDA** *enters. She watches him, mustering up the courage to wake him.*)

(*Finally:*)

IDA. (*Scared.*) Excuse me.

(*Nothing.*)

Hey.

Excuse me.

(*Nothing.*)

Damn, are you dead?

Excuse me.

(**KLASS** *wakes up. Looks at* **IDA.** **IDA** *looks at* **KLASS.**)

Hey, I didn't mean to wake you up.

But –

but you have my –

(**KLASS** *screams.*)

(**IDA** *screams.*)

(**KLASS** *jumps up on the bench, screaming.*)

(**IDA** *runs away, screaming.*)

Afternoon

(**KLASS** *is perched on the bench, just like* **IDA**
*was at the top of the play. He uses a worn
sheet of newspaper to polish a metal coffee
pot.*)

(**IDA** *enters, carrying a reconfigured wire
hanger. She holds it out as a weapon for self
defense.*)

(*She announces herself:*)

IDA. Excuse me.

(**KLASS** *looks up.*)

Hey!

(**KLASS** *looks at* **IDA.**)

You got something that belongs to me.

(**KLASS** *goes back to polishing his coffee pot.*)

Look, I don't wanna have to call the police.

(**KLASS** *stops polishing.*)

Yeah, man, you heard Thick Necks fryin' sane brothas
so you know they'd blaze your crazy ass up.

(**KLASS** *looks at* **IDA** *then returns to polishing
his pot.*)

Those are my keys
you got
on your wrist.
I want those back.
You can act all types of stupid after you give me back
what's mine.

(**KLASS** *carefully places the pot on the ground.*
IDA *assumes he's going for her keys, but
instead he takes a drinking glass from the
crate and wipes it clean.*)

You just gonna sit there

like I'm not even talking to you?

> (**KLASS** *places the glass next to the coffee pot.*
> *Takes out a spoon and wipes it.*)

My man gets off from work soon.

I was trying to do you a favor and handle all this on my own without involving him.

I told him you screamed at me.

You remember that from this morning?

Hollering at me like you a damn terrorist!

You remember that shit?

He was not happy to hear you flipped out on me.

So, I would suggest you pull your screws together long enough to do the right thing.

> (**KLASS** *stops polishing. Sticks the spoon in the drinking glass.*)
>
> (*He looks at* **IDA**.)
>
> (**IDA** *looks at* **KLASS**. *Grips the wire hanger.*)
>
> (**KLASS** *gets off the bench. Goes inside his coat, digs.*)
>
> (**IDA** *panics, thinking he's got a gun. She hits the floor, covering her head.*)
>
> (**KLASS** *pulls out a white feather. Holds it out to* **IDA**. *Her keys dangle from his wrist.*)
>
> (**IDA** *uncovers her head when no shots ring out. She looks up. Sees her keys.*)

Those are mine.

See?

You're wearing my keys.

> (*She gets up. Stops when she sees the feather.*)
>
> (**KLASS** *looks at her. A slight smirk on his face.*)
>
> (**IDA** *looks at her keys...or the feather.*)
>
> (**KLASS** *holds the feather out for* **IDA** *to take.*)

(**IDA** *looks at him, taking in his features for the first time.*)

How old are you?

You look young.

Might even be younger than Wynn.

(**KLASS** *drops the feather, returns to the bench.*)

(**IDA** *catches the feather as it falls.*)

(**KLASS** *picks up his pot, polishes it.*)

(*She watches him.*)

All the drug heads and street crazies around here are old men

with grey hair and tight skin. They stink. And they fidget.

That's not like you.

(*She holds up the feather.*)

Where'd you find this?

KLASS. =.=

IDA. I see crows sometimes.

I look up and I see crows soaring.

Wynn says I'm crazy.

Didn't know we had birds like this. (*Re: the feather.*)

=.=

Can I have my keys?

Please?

My mama's gonna know something's up if I stay out two nights in a row.

(**KLASS** *carefully places the coffee pot back in the crate.*)

I'm sorry I came at you with that hanger.

I wasn't gonna use it.

I don't do that.

I don't hurt people.

(**KLASS** *looks at* **IDA**.*)*

IDA. I don't wanna make this a thing.

Don't want to call the police unless I have to.

I need my keys back.

(**KLASS** *picks up the drinking glass with the spoon in it, puts both things back in the crate.)*

(*He tucks the crate under the bench.)*

(*He sits down. Folds his arms so that the wrist with the keys attached is tucked under his other arm, pressed against his body.)*

(**KLASS** *falls asleep.)*

(**IDA** *watches him.)*

(*To herself.)* I don't believe this shit.

No he didn't just sit up here and fall asleep...

Evening

(That same day.)

*(No **KLASS**, but his crate is still tucked under the bench.)*

*(**IDA** enters with **WYNN**.)*

IDA. Mr. Wheeler said he's been gone for a few hours.

WYNN. We should take his crate.

He got your keys; we take his shit.

Negotiate a swap.

IDA. I don't want that junk.

WYNN. It's leverage.

IDA. I don't need leverage. I need keys. I haveta go home tonight.

Haveta tell my mama what the deal is so she can blow up about spending money to get the locks changed. Again.

WYNN. Maybe this is a sign, Ida.

IDA. What?

WYNN. Maybe all this came together

to make us take things to the next level.

IDA. "All this"...? All of what?

WYNN. Your crazy mama.

Pigeon Man.

You losing your keys.

All this disruption is bringing us closer together.

IDA. It is?

WYNN. It is.

Or...it could.

If we let it.

All these signs are hooking up

to tell us we should be living together.

IDA. I didn't see any signs getting down like that.

WYNN. Your mama's gonna tell you to walk right back out when you tell her why she had to unlock the door for you.

IDA. *(Hadn't considered this.)* You think she'd kick me out??

WYNN. She might.

But if you decide to live with me, it won't matter what she says to you.

IDA. She's not gonna kick me out.

WYNN. She's got a temper.

IDA. She needs my help.

WYNN. That day nurse been handling most of the work.

IDA. She wouldn't throw // me out.

I'm her only child.

WYNN. And you know who's gonna be there when she tosses you?

=.= *(Me! Ta-da!)*

IDA. I haveta get those keys back.

WYNN. You don't think it's a sign?

IDA. Have you seen him *(Re:* **KLASS**.*)* around here before?

WYNN. Ida, I asked you a question.

IDA. I asked you a question, Wynn.

WYNN. =.=

IDA. =.=

WYNN. No.

I haven't seen Pigeon Man before. //

Now you gonna answer mine?

IDA. Don't call him Pigeon Man.

WYNN. Would you listen to me?!

IDA. He's your age.

WYNN. Who?

(Points at the crate.)

IDA. He is.

I think y'all around the same age.

WYNN. No way, man.

IDA. I looked him in the face.

He got that beard, but there's a baby face under it.

He's young.

WYNN. Wouldn't no dude my age *choose* to be like that.

IDA. Who said it's a choice?

WYNN. You comparing him to me?

IDA. I'm not.

WYNN. I hope not.

IDA. He makes me think of Antonio...

My daddy, too. A lil bit.

WYNN. Your daddy ain't homeless.

Neither is Antonio.

IDA. That's not what I'm sayin', Wynn.

WYNN. Then what?

IDA. Nevermind...

=.=

You think the cops got him?

WYNN. They would've taken his stuff.

=.=

=.=

> (**WYNN** *takes out his wallet.*)
>
> (*He pulls out a few bills and a business card.*)

Here.

IDA. What's this for?

WYNN. *(Re: the business card.)* I went to school with him.
He's a locksmith now.

Got his own business.

Tell him you're with me, and he'll give you a discount.

You pay him that much.

IDA. Wynn, I don't wanna take –

WYNN. Your mama can't bust you up if you already got a
solution to the problem.

> (**IDA** *takes in* **WYNN**'s *gesture.*)
>
> (*She kisses him as a sign of gratitude.*)
>
> (*He hugs her to seal the deal.*)
>
> (*While embracing an oblivious* **WYNN**, **IDA**
> *looks to the crate...*)

Night

(Rain.)

(The bench is empty.)

(The crate remains.)

(Suddenly, the slim beam of a flashlight appears.)

*(**IDA** enters, carrying an umbrella and shining a flashlight.)*

(She carries a black trash bag.)

(She crosses to the crate, puts down the umbrella, pulls the crate from underneath the bench, and attempts to wrap the trash bag around it.)

*(**KLASS** enters.)*

KLASS. What are you doin' with my stuff?

*(**IDA** jumps up, falls back.)*

IDA. It's raining.

KLASS. I know it's raining.

IDA. Your stuff was getting wet.

KLASS. You trying to steal my crate?

IDA. No! No I'm not I wasn't I'm not I'm I was wrapping that bag around it.

'Cause, 'cause, I know you take all that time polishing your pot and your glass.

KLASS. How you know that? You watching me?

IDA. I came here. I been here. I talked to you.

Been talking to you. I'm the one you gave the feather to. You got my keys on your wrist.

*(**KLASS** looks at his wrist. The keys dangle.)*

*(He looks at **IDA**.)*

(He sits.)

KLASS. You keeping my stuff dry?

(**IDA** *scrambles for her umbrella.*)

IDA. Yeah.

KLASS. Why?

IDA. I figured you have important things in there.

KLASS. =.=

IDA. =.=

KLASS. (*Slow realization.*) You taking care of my crate...?

IDA. Yeah for real.

No lie.

(**KLASS** *studies* **IDA.**)

(*She watches him study her.*)

(**KLASS** *stands. Faces* **IDA.**)

(*He removes the keys from his wrist.*)

(*Holds them out for* **IDA** *to take.*)

(*She inches toward him.*)

(*She reaches out to take the keys from* **KLASS.**)

(*There's the slightest pause for a shared breath.*)

(*Just as* **IDA** *clasps her hand around the keys,* **KLASS** *grabs her.* **IDA** *drops the umbrella.*)

(*He holds her... [Is it a hug or squeeze?]* **IDA** *is silenced as she struggles to break free.*)

(*Suddenly, quiet noise pops from* **IDA.** **KLASS** *releases her as swiftly as he grabbed her.*)

(*She runs away, leaving the umbrella on the ground.*)

(**KLASS** *watches her run.*)

(*He crosses to his crate. Finishes wrapping the trash bag around it.*)

(*He takes the umbrella. Sits. Props it up to protect himself from the rain.*)

(**KLASS** *sleeps.*)

Day

(The benches are empty. The crate is gone.)

*(**IDA** enters, carrying plastic bags full of groceries. The closer she gets to the benches, the faster she walks. She avoids looking at them. She crosses the courtyard. Exits.)*

Evening

(**WYNN**, *perched on a bench, is in the middle of telling a story to a group of people unseen by the audience.* **WYNN** *isn't as good as* **IDA**, *but he enjoys the attention.*)

(**IDA** *keeps close to* **WYNN**, *almost unable to stand near the spot where the earlier incident with* **KLASS** *occurred. She's distracted, avoids eye contact.*)

WYNN. ...Antonio had a seizure in the holding cell. They had to take him to the hospital.

He's in a coma, but they still got him in shackles though, got him handcuffed to the bed.

He had a warrant. Missed a court date. That's why they arrested him.

This dude who works at the hospital brought his car into the shop this afternoon.

Told me the whole deal. The news don't even know about it, that's how recent it is.

But I don't think the news care one way or the other.

They don't talk about brothas minding they own business, getting shook down.

They want a big, loud, crazy muthafucka waving around a switchblade.

Ida, you heard anything on the news?

IDA. No.

WYNN. See?

And Ida been sitting up in her apartment steady watching TV like it's her job.

Like she on some quest for that six-figure salary type shit –

(**IDA** *smacks* **WYNN** *on the arm. Hard.*)

Yo, what the fuck?

IDA. Don't go around talking about how I spend my time.

WYNN. What you hit me for?

IDA. I didn't hear anything about Antonio, okay?
No need to tell people what I do.

WYNN. What's wrong with you?

IDA. I'm going back up.

> (**IDA** *goes to exit.* **WYNN** *goes after her.*)

WYNN. *(Grabbing her.)* Wait a minute –

IDA. Don't touch me.

WYNN. What's wrong with you?

IDA. I don't feel like being outside.

WYNN. You bust me in my arm 'cause you hate being outside?

IDA. Fucking neighborhood stinks in the summer.
All this heat. // I don't like being out.

WYNN. Why'd you hit me in front of everybody?

IDA. Don't matter anyway. Everybody sees everything, but they don't care.
Everybody is always out, in the streets. Day and night.
People on stoops, leaning on cars, hanging out of windows.
You can't get away from nobody.
Building one: (**IDA** *turns in the direction of the first building.*) see?
There's Mr. Wheeler smoking up, reading the paper.
Building three: *(Turns in the direction of the third building.)* Sasha is on the phone running her mouth.
Building four: *(Turns.)* Mrs. James is greasing her scalp.
Building two: *(Turns.)* my mama is sitting up there sleeping.

WYNN. Ida, what the hell are you // talking about?

IDA. Four buildings make up this project.
And every building got seven floors.
And every floor got eleven windows going across it.
All those windows facing down to this courtyard, those benches.

So Mr. Wheeler was smoking.

So Sasha was talking bullshit.

Mrs. James was sitting by the window, listening to the radio.

But nobody said nothing to me.

Nobody asked me anything.

Am I crazy?

I don't know if I'm crazy. Don't know if I'm making shit up.

WYNN. Ida –

IDA. Am I cracking out?

Sitting up in my dingy ass apartment, hiding out from what? From who?

Something I made up? Must've. Had to have made it up 'cause nobody said nothing.

It wasn't nothing.

Nothing for me to sprint pass these benches everyday.

This is the only way out to the street, Wynn.

When I leave my building I have to cross through here to get to the street.

Every other exit is blocked by a fence with a thick chain and fat padlock keeping it shut.

I can't even choose how I come and go.

WYNN. Ida, did something happen to you?

IDA. I'm glad I met you downtown at a movie theater.

Nowhere near here 'cause otherwise I'd only see all this *(Re: the projects.)* when I look at you.

But I don't. I don't, Wynn. And that's why I like you. That's why I need you.

=.=

=.=

I'm going home.

I'll talk to you later.

(**IDA** *exits, leaving* **WYNN** *speechless.*)

Day

(Neighborhood sounds bounce around the
space.)

(The crate is back.)

(**KLASS** is back.)

(He sits on the ground, fiddling with an
upright vacuum cleaner on its side.)

(The hood on his coat is removed from his
head. This is the first moment we see **KLASS**'
face in the daylight.)

(**WYNN** enters, carrying a small gift bag
[a gift for **IDA**]. He stops short when he sees
KLASS.)

(On his cell phone:)

WYNN. Yeah, I'm outside.
Okay. Bye.

(**WYNN** hangs up.)

(Watches **KLASS**.)

Hey, man, how old are you?

KLASS. =.=

WYNN. I'm twenty-seven.
My girl thinks you're my age.
I don't think so though...
Good job giving back those keys.
I woulda had to fuck you up if she didn't get those keys
back.
Nothing personal.
I mean, I had other plans for me and her, but she wanted
her keys
and I try to do what makes her happy.

KLASS. That's good.

WYNN. Yeah. It is.

KLASS. Nothing personal.

WYNN. Nothing personal.

=.=

=.=

Hey, what's wrong with you, man?

Why you out here, sitting under this hot ass sun wearing a coat?

KLASS. =.=

WYNN. Alright.

Cool.

I understand.

I need to mind my own.

Cool.

=.=

You trying to fix that?

What's wrong with it?

KLASS. I think something's wrong with the motor.

WYNN. I used to repair shit like that.

I'd bust open a blender or a iron or a fuckin' vacuum

and it'd just come to me. I could figure out what didn't look right

and then go in and fix it.

I could see how it needed to be so it would work.

Then I went to automotive school.

You been to school?

KLASS. No.

WYNN. I finished school. Been set ever since.

I decided I had a skill, and I figured out how to make money off of it.

And I'm taking care of myself, too.

People need cars to get where they need to go.

And they need people like me to make sure those cars keep going.

I want one of those city jobs, working on the buses.

That's money. Me and Ida be set for life.

(**KLASS** *stops working on the vacuum when he hears* **IDA***'s name.*)

(*He looks at* **WYNN**. **WYNN** *looks at* **KLASS**.)

(**KLASS** *returns to the vacuum.*)

WYNN. You can still probably get your shit together. You got time.

If you good enough at fixing things, you could get a decent job.

Be a super or something.

(**KLASS** *stops working, looks at* **WYNN**.)

You don't have the right tools if you trying to fix that though.

I'd let you borrow some of mine but my shit is too nice.

Plus, I don't know you from that bench.

=.=

What's your name?

KLASS. What's your name?

WYNN. =.=

=.=

Wynn.

KLASS. =.=

=.=

Klass.

WYNN. Class? Like in "classroom"?

KLASS. Yea but it starts with a "K."

(**KLASS** *extends his arm to bump fists with* **WYNN**.*)

(**WYNN** *hesitates but eventually leans over and bumps fists with* **KLASS**.*)

(*Each man sees his reflection in the other man's eyes.*)

(*It's an awkward moment that shows* **WYNN***'s uneasiness and* **KLASS***' stillness.*)

*(If we had any doubt of who's in control, we
assume from this gesture it's probably **KLASS**.)*

*(**KLASS** goes back to the vacuum.)*

WYNN. You do look young.

=.=

I could be you. You could be me. You never know how
these things end up.

We both could be that brotha Antonio. You hear about
that? That shit is crazy.

But the cops probably harass you all the time.

You used to that shit, ain't you?

KLASS. =.=

WYNN. You picked a good spot, hanging here.

Those Thick Necks that patrol here are hired to
"contain" not "prevent."

Hey, did you see anything go down recently?

KLASS. =.=

WYNN. I think something happened to my girl,

but she's not talking about it.

I asked around. Nobody's claiming to see anything.

KLASS. *(Working on the vacuum.)* I can't remember.

WYNN. You can't remember or you don't?

KLASS. I can't.

I'm not sure.

I don't know.

I don't.

Remember.

WYNN. =.=

KLASS. =.=

*(**WYNN** studies **KLASS**.)*

WYNN. Well, if you hear anything

or

if you see anybody that's not right.

Let me know.

I'm over here a lot with Ida.

KLASS. If I see something that's not right, you'll be the first person I say something to.

Night

(Two crates of junk and a vacuum cleaner.)

*(**KLASS** plays the feather game.)*

(He sits on a bench, holding out a white feather.)

(He aims for a glass that sits between his feet on the ground.)

(He lets go of the feather.)

(It lands in the glass...or it doesn't.)

(He picks the feather up.)

(Aims it.)

(Lets go.)

(In the glass...or not.)

(He picks the feather up.)

(Aims it.)

(Lets go...)

Morning

(**KLASS** *has a small pocket radio up to his ear.*)

(*Quiet, muffled voices seep from its tiny speaker.*)

(*Maybe it's reggae or jazz.*)

(**KLASS** *paces, circling the bench.*)

(**IDA** *enters, crosses the space, trying to walk by unnoticed.*)

(*Just as she passes him* **KLASS** *registers it's her.*)

KLASS. Excuse me...

(**IDA** *ignores him.*)

(*She exits.*)

Evening

(Two crates full of junk, a vacuum, and a pile of brightly-colored summer dresses.)

*(**KLASS** sits on the pile of dresses, polishing his coffee pot.)*

*(**IDA** crosses.)*

KLASS. *(A quiet melody.)* Ida Ida Ida Ida Ida...

*(**IDA** ignores him, exits.)*

Afternoon

(Rain.)

*(**KLASS** wraps all of his things in trash bags.)*

(He sits under Ida's umbrella. Unfazed by Mother Nature's tears.)

Night

(**KLASS** *has found a pen and a notebook with Destiny's Child on the cover.*)

(*On sheet after sheet he writes and draws and writes and draws and writes and draws...*)

(*This is a moment of confession for* **KLASS**. *Filling each page provides a painful relief that causes him to sway, pace, and occasionally shake out a nagging cramp in his writing hand. This is the first time he's put these words and images on paper.*)

Day

> *(Two crates full of junk, a vacuum cleaner, a pile of dresses, and an old floor lamp without the lamp shade.)*
>
> *(**KLASS** sits on the ground, looks up at the sky, daydreaming.)*
>
> *(He holds the notebook against his chest.)*
>
> *(Beyonce, et al. smile out at the audience.)*
>
> *(**IDA** enters.)*
>
> *(**KLASS** sees that it's **IDA**. He jumps up on the bench and holds out the notebook.)*

KLASS. Excuse me.

> *(**IDA** keeps walking.)*

Excuse me, this is for you...Ida.
I found this for you.

> *(**KLASS** leaps off the bench and into **IDA**'s path.)*
>
> *(She stops short with a slight gasp.)*
>
> *(She looks around her. Is anyone noticing this?)*

Someone threw it out. But I caught it.
Saved it. For you.

> *(**KLASS** holds the notebook up to her.)*
>
> *(He looks at her.)*
>
> *(She looks at him.)*
>
> *(Sounds of the neighborhood peak.)*

It's for you.
I left parts of it blank
so
you could fill it with things about yourself.
I wrote about me. I tell you about me.

You see that? *(Points to the cover.)*
That's... *(As if saying a foreign word.)* Destiny's Child,
but I got it because of the sky behind them.
I like their sky because it feels big.
It looks like it can hold a lot. That sky.
When I sit here and I look up.
Our sky looks so empty.
Saggy and limp.
Looks like it couldn't hold anything I try to put up there.
Too flimsy to hold any dream or idea or or possibility.
But... Destiny's Child's sky is so full.
It could hold anything you need to keep.

> *(**IDA** studies the cover of the notebook.)*
>
> *(Then she looks up, studies the sky above them.)*
>
> *(Then she looks at **KLASS**.)*
>
> *(He's right.)*
>
> *(**KLASS** places the notebook on the ground, then steps back. He looks to **IDA**.)*
>
> *(**IDA** looks at **KLASS**. She looks at the notebook. She's cautious. Crosses over and picks it up.)*

Evening

(**KLASS** *sits on the ground, polishing a set of salt & pepper shakers.*)

(*The pocket radio rests next to him.*)

(*Jazz music squirms out of the tiny speaker.*)

(**IDA** *sits on the bench, reading through the notebook.*)

(*She comes across something that's shocking or disgusting.*)

(*She looks at* **KLASS**, *who's concentrating on his shakers.*)

(*Considers asking him about what she just read.*)

(*Decides against it.*)

(*Returns to reading.*)

(*Turns the page.*)

(*Reads.*)

(*She laughs out loud, covers her mouth.*)

(*Looks at* **KLASS**, *slightly embarrassed. He doesn't notice.*)

(*She returns to reading.*)

Day

(Two crates full of junk, a vacuum cleaner, a pile of dresses, an old floor lamp without the lamp shade, and a wooden footstool.)

*(**KLASS** sits on the footstool, stacking primary-colored saucers in the form of a pyramid.)*

*(**IDA** sits on the bench with a glass between her feet. She plays the feather game while she talks.)*

(The sounds of the neighborhood bump.)

IDA. My mama says I need to start helping with the rent.

She wants me to pay for things now that I'm done with school.

I told her I'm not done. Said I'm thinking about community college.

She said I can think about that while I'm working at a job.

But I don't know where I would work though.

Maybe I should just move in with Wynn.

That could be fun.

He'd probably pay for me to go to school, too.

It helped him get where he is.

KLASS. =.=

IDA. I like sitting here with you.

I like it because, because it's quiet.

It feels quiet with you.

=.=

=.=

I finished reading your part of the sky last night.

I finished your pages.

Is all that stuff you wrote for real?

All that really happened to you?

KLASS. =.=

=.=

Yes.

> (*This lands heavy against* **IDA**.)
>
> (*She looks at* **KLASS**, *who doesn't look at her.*)
>
> (*He keeps his gaze on the bright colors of the saucer.*)
>
> (**IDA** *returns to the feather game.*)

IDA. You used to live here. In building one.

KLASS. =.=

IDA. You got people that still live here?

KLASS. I don't know.

IDA. You should look for 'em.

They probably don't recognize you.

Practically live in that big ass coat.

They probably walk past you everyday and don't realize you're a part of the family.

KLASS. (*Wanting to change the subject.*) That dude died.

IDA. What dude?

> (**KLASS** *makes a zap sound.*)

Antonio?

How'd you find that out?

KLASS. I woke up last night saw it in the sky.

> (**IDA** *looks up at the sky above them.*)

IDA. What'd you see in the sky?

KLASS. A crow. Circling.

IDA. (*Looks at* **KLASS**.) At night?

KLASS. At night.

That's how I knew.

And then I was getting these (*Re: the saucers.*) when I heard people talking about it.

IDA. Where'd you get all this shit from?

KLASS. I found it.

IDA. You stealing it?

KLASS. No.

People throw away things they don't want.
I catch it.

IDA. People already call you Pigeon,
they see all this and gonna add "shit" to it.
You want everybody calling you Pigeon Shit?

(**KLASS** *smiles. He laughs. He thinks it's funny.*)

It's not funny, Klass.
You want people talking about you like that?

(**KLASS** *starts to coo like a pigeon.*)

(*He laughs. Makes shit sounds with his mouth.*)

(*He laughs.*)

That's digusting!

(*But* **IDA** *starts laughing, too.*)

(**KLASS** *coos again. He walks like a pigeon, scooting around the bench.*)

(**IDA** *laughs. She holds out the feather.*)

(**KLASS** *takes it, perches on the bench next to her.*)

(*He places the feather in her hair.*)

(*He coos.*)

(**WYNN** *enters.*)

WYNN. Ida!

IDA. Wynn!

(**KLASS** *coos a hello.*)

WYNN. Ida, do I have to bust Klass in the face?

IDA. No!

(**IDA** *pushes* **KLASS** *away.*)

(*He rolls off the bench, springs to his feet.*)

(*Dusts himself off, then returns to the footstool.*)

(*He polishes his saucers.*)

WYNN. Why are you sitting out here? With him? Like this!
　　You remember all that counting you did?
　　Seven floors, eleven windows? Everybody can see.

IDA. We were just talking.
　　Nobody's paying attention –

WYNN. What are you two talking about?

IDA. Antonio died.

WYNN. I know.
　　He already told you that?

IDA. Yeah.

WYNN. I was coming to tell you that.

IDA. You still can.

WYNN. Don't act like I'm a kid, Ida.

IDA. Nobody's treating you // like a kid.

WYNN. *(Re: the feather in her hair.)* And what's that?

IDA. This?

WYNN. He pulled that from some bird
　　and the only birds around here are those nasty ass
　　pigeons.

IDA. It's white.
　　White pigeons are doves.

WYNN. He told you that, too.

IDA. Yes.

WYNN. This is some cracked out shit.

IDA. What are you doing here, Wynn?
　　You're supposed to be at work.

WYNN. People telling me you been hanging out with pigeons.

IDA. I been talking with Klass.

WYNN. I'm taking you to lunch.
　　I'm on my lunch break.
　　I'm coming to take you out for some food.

IDA. I'm not hungry.

WYNN. Well then come watch me eat.

IDA. I don't want to.

WYNN. I'm taking you to lunch.

IDA. I'm not going anywhere.

WYNN. Ida, come on!

> (**WYNN** *grabs* **IDA**'s *arm, but she escapes his grasp.*)
>
> (*They look at each other.*)
>
> (**KLASS** *looks at them.*)

You wanna sit up here with this fuck
instead of spending time with me?

IDA. I didn't say that.

WYNN. You actin' like it.

IDA. Don't grab me like that.

WYNN. You want me to rub some dirty ass feather all over
you?
Is that it?

IDA. Don't grab me again.

WYNN. Don't *make* me grab you.

> (*He steps toward her.*)
>
> (**IDA** *dares him to come closer.*)
>
> (**WYNN** *backs down.*)

Whatever, Ida.

You find me when you get your shit together.

> (**WYNN** *exits.*)
>
> (**IDA** *watches him walk away, rubbing her arm.*)
>
> (**IDA** *looks to* **KLASS**, *who picks up a saucer and starts polishing it.*)

Night

*(No **KLASS**.)*

(Two crates full of junk, a vacuum cleaner, a pile of dresses, an old floor lamp without the lamp shade, and a footstool.)

*(**IDA**'s stretched out on the pile of dresses, looking up at the sky.)*

(A pen pokes out of her mouth.)

*(Hip-hop music thumps in the distance, but **IDA** rests as if she's in a serene meadow.)*

*(The Destiny's Child notebook is open, resting against **IDA**'s hip. We see a block of text scribbled across the top half of the page.)*

*(Suddenly, **IDA** sits up, grabs the notebook, and writes, writes, writes.)*

(A man yells in the distance, sirens, a woman wails, dogs bark.)

Evening

(Two crates full of junk, a vacuum cleaner, a pile of dresses, an old floor lamp without the lamp shade, a footstool, and a bathroom sink.)

*(**KLASS** is asleep on the bench.)*

*(**IDA** enters with a McDonald's bag and the notebook.)*

(She places both items next to him. Exits.)

Night

> (**KLASS** *is asleep on top of the dresses. He grips the sleeve of a dress, wrestling with demons in his sleep. Grunts leap from his throat. He wakes with a jump and scampers across the ground.*)

KLASS. Get away from me!

Get away from me!

Get back!

> (*He scoots away from his invisible predator, running to the bench as if it were a haven. He climbs atop the bench, grabs a can opener, holds it like a weapon. His words are wrapped in fear. It should be clear he can't follow through on any of the following threats:*)

Don't touch me! Don't touch me! You touch me, you get your nuts snatched!!

Touch me and you get your face fucked with a razor dick!

Choke your throat with rusted nails, punk bitch!

Make sure you shit needles, muthafucka!

> (**KLASS** *drops the can opener.*)

(*Whimpers.*) Please...

> (*He slumps into a ball.*)

Please...

Please...don't.

> (*Buries his face. Heavy breath.*)

Morning

(Hot.)

(Real hot.)

(The floor lamp and vacuum cleaner are gone.)

*(**KLASS** has unzipped his coat. It's spread open to reveal his wiry frame dressed in a white tank top and baggy khakis.)*

*(**IDA** shoots him with a water gun. He doesn't react to the hits.)*

IDA. This isn't even doin' anything.

Are you sure you getting cooler?

KLASS. =.=

IDA. Shit, it's too hot to play crazy with that coat.

(She shoots him.)

Don't you think you'll feel a little...lighter if you take that shit off.

*(She strolls gangsta-style on **KLASS**, shooting him from different spots around the bench.)*

(Menace II Society-*esque.*) What's up now, pot-nuh?!

*(**IDA** pulls the trigger several times. **KLASS** doesn't flinch.)*

*(**IDA** drops the water gun and transforms into the wailing mother often seen in 90s gangsta flicks: exaggerated, loud, uncontrolled.)*

Oh gawd!!

Oh lawd!! Ricki!!!

*(**IDA** fake sobs, cradling **KLASS**' head against her bosom.)*

(Screaming to no one in particular:)

You did this to him!!

(This phrase triggers something in **KLASS***. Panic and worry slowly conquer his face. It's as if he's slowly stepping into a painful memory.)*

*(***IDA*** doesn't notice this. Continues her performance.)*

IDA. You...did...this...to... *(Losing her breath.)*
MY BABY!!

KLASS. I'm sorry.

*(***IDA*** is still wrapped in her performance.)*

IDA. Baby, I'm sorry too, baby!!

*(***KLASS*** clings to* **IDA***.)*

KLASS. I'm sorry. I'm sorry.

*(***KLASS*** buries his face in her bosom. He cries.)*

IDA. Are you cryin' for real?

*(***KLASS***' cry turns into a weep.)*

Klass, what's wrong?

*(***KLASS*** climbs on the bench. Perches on the seat. Never losing physical contact with* **IDA***.)*

I can't help if you don't tell me what's wrong –

*(***KLASS*** wraps his arms around* **IDA***.)*

(He squeezes **IDA***.)*

(A weak sound escapes from her body due to the pressure.)

Klass, that's too tight.

(He weeps. Squeezes **IDA** *tighter.)*

(Strained.) Klass...

KLASS. I'm sorry, Mama. I'm sorry sorry sorry I couldn't save you. I'm sorry...

Day

(Two crates full of junk, a pile of dresses, a footstool, a bathroom sink, and a yellow rug.)

(Several fliers are tacked to both benches.)

*(**KLASS** is asleep.)*

*(**IDA** enters wearing a T-shirt that reads "To Protect & Serve Who?" on the front.)*

(A picture of a young Black man [Antonio] is printed on the back.)

(The years 1982–2008 are printed under the picture.)

*(**IDA** chants:)*

IDA. Justice for our Streets!!
Justice means Peace!!

> *(**KLASS** wakes with a start. He looks at **IDA**. Has she lost her mind?)*

Justice for our Streets!!
Justice means Peace!!

> *(Spoken:)*

Klass,
oh my god,
Klass you shoulda seen it!
People everywhere!
Signs everywhere!
Speeches!
Chants!
Shit, I should protest more often.
I feel good!!

> *(Idea!)*

You should start one.
You should make a sign
then

go down and call out those ignorant muthafuckas sittin'
in those big offices.
Shame those ignorant money whores who are only
interested in helping A people
not THE people, you know?
They only interested in a certain kind of people
who don't LOOK nothin' like me or you.
Who don't LIVE like me or you.
ESPECIALLY you.
Go down there and bust some knowledge in the face of
those dudes who makin' your life
so hard. Got you out here livin' like this.
We need to get you down there, Klass.

    (Wait a minute.)

But, but you need a chant though.
We need to write a good one for you.
You gotta yell something in repetition. Make it have a
rhythm to it.
Not too many words.
Gotta be simple and to the point.
So those cash hoes know what you saying.
They gotta know what you're willing to do for your
rights. For your justice.
It's gotta be short
'cause the more you say your chant,
the more you believe it.
You start yelling it. Getting loud!!
And you feel it coming from your toes, your nose, your,
your lips, your eyeballs:
Justice for our Streets!!
Justice means Peace!!

    (This is how it's going down:)

I'll make signs.
One for me. One for you.

And T-shirts.

We can make those together.

We'll make T-shirts.

These *(Re: the one she's wearing.)* cost ten bucks or some shit.

We'll make some T-shirts.

We'll go in the streets

and keep marching and chanting 'til they right the wrongs!

KLASS. But I don't wanna yell.

I don't got nothin' to yell about.

IDA. Yeah you do.

You got plenty of things to protest.

You wanna keep livin' like this?

KLASS. What's wrong with it?

IDA. What's wrong with it?

Are you serious?

You see anybody fightin' to get a spot on this bench?

KLASS. You.

IDA. =.=

=.=

I don't wanna live on a damn bench, okay?

Don't get all stinked with me. I'm talking about helping you.

KLASS. You woke me up.

IDA. Go back to sleep then.

KLASS. You woke me up, talking some mess, and now I can't go back to sleep.

IDA. Some mess?

A Black man died, Klass.

At the hands of some Thick Necks.

You should be upset about that.

KLASS. Why?

IDA. Hel-low!

Black Man!

That's you!

They could snag you just like they did Antonio.

KLASS. He was selling fake handbags.

It's against the law.

IDA. Folks sell fake everything on that block.

All year round.

The cops don't do anything about it

until they have to meet a ticket quote.

KLASS. Quota.

IDA. What?

KLASS. Ticket "quota."

IDA. Are you correcting how I speak?

KLASS. Maybe you should take notes at the next one.

Get it right.

IDA. Maybe you should watch how you talk to me.

KLASS. =.=

> (**KLASS** *jumps up,* **IDA** *jumps back.*)
>
> (*He rips the fliers from the bench.*)

And don't put

this shit

on my stuff.

IDA. It's public property –

KLASS. It's MY property.

And I don't want pictures of a DEAD MAN

hanging on MY property.

IDA. I can hang whatever I want all over this damn bench.

It belongs to the buildings and the people who live in

those buildings.

That's me. Not you. Me.

KLASS. Oh, so, it's my property when you wanna sit up here

and watch the sky? When you fightin' with your boyfriend

or

mad at your mama?

Post this shit where somebody gives a fuck.

And find your own shit to protest, Ida.

I don't need you protesting for me.

> (**KLASS** *angrily shifts his weight on the bench to try and go back to sleep.* **IDA** *stands, speechless.*)
>
> (*She quietly picks up the fliers that* **KLASS** *ripped off.*)
>
> (*She looks at him. Anger swelling but unable to say anything.*)
>
> (*She exits.*)

Night

(All of Klass' things [two crates full of junk, a pile of dresses, etc.] are neatly packed under both benches.)

(KLASS holds the pocket radio up to his ear.)

(Quiet, muffled voices seep from its small speaker.)

(He circles the bench. Head down.)

(IDA enters, stops just at the edge.)

(WYNN follows. He stands next to her.)

(He grabs her hand in defiance.)

(They cross in front of the bench.)

(KLASS doesn't break his pattern around the bench. He doesn't look up.)

(IDA looks at KLASS. WYNN tugs.)

(IDA and WYNN exit. KLASS watches them walk away.)

Night

(Rain.)

(Ida's umbrella is broken.)

*(***KLASS*** *sits on the footstool. He removes his coat and wraps it around the notebook.)*

Evening

(Two crates full of junk, a pile of dresses, a footstool, a bathroom sink, a yellow rug, and a bicycle wheel with the u-lock still attached.)

(All of Klass' things remain neatly packed under both benches.)

(No **KLASS**.*)*

*(***WYNN*** and* **IDA** *are by the benches.)*

WYNN. You talk to your mama, yet?

IDA. No.

She's gonna say it's a bad idea.

WYNN. Then she's wrong.

It's a good idea.

A great idea.

Best thing I heard all week.

All year.

All my life.

IDA. I've been thinking about it for awhile.

WYNN. Couldn't ignore the signs any longer?

IDA. That's right.

WYNN. I'm glad, Ida.

I felt like I was the last thing on your mind.

It's nice to hear you been thinking about it.

It's hard to know when somebody's considering an idea.

You haven't been treatin' me like you been considering me.

IDA. You haven't been treatin' me like a consideration either.

WYNN. =.=

=.=

I don't wanna put my hands on you.

IDA. I know.

WYNN. I shouldn't.

IDA. You won't. Not again.

WYNN. I won't.

And you won't hang out with Pigeon.

IDA. His name is Klass.

WYNN. You won't.

IDA. I shouldn't.

WYNN. Not again.

No more.

IDA. I shouldn't.

WYNN. You thinkin' they *(Re: the building's tenants.)* don't see.

They see you.

IDA. There's a difference between seeing and recognizing.

A difference between watching and looking.

WYNN. Don't P and Q this talk, Ida.

IDA. Nobody cares, Wynn.

WYNN. Your mama knows you hanging out with him?

IDA. Yeah.

WYNN. What she saying?

IDA. She yells about it.

WYNN. Are you listening?

IDA. I hear it. Don't listen.

WYNN. You should be listenin'.

IDA. Maybe I'll listen when she says I'm not ready to move in with you.

WYNN. No. Don't listen to that part.

You might hear it, but don't listen to her.

He's crazy. I'm not.

IDA. He's not crazy –

WYNN. If I have to grab you

and take you away from him,

I'll do that.

I'll snatch you from this to save you.

IDA. From what?

WYNN. =.= *(How do I say this?)*

You're not the kind of female
who saves people.
You can't fix him.
You can't fix people.
You settle into how they are.
That's why I'm good for you,
'cause I got my shit together.
And me having my shit together
means you'll have yourself together, too.

IDA. It's hard for me to see the good in what you just said.

WYNN. It's in there.
I want to help you.
I want your dreams to come true.
Shake you from playing pretend with Pigeon.
You think he's gonna save you?
You see what kind of situation he got his self in.
What you want for yourself, Ida?
I'll make sure you get it.

> (**IDA** *thinks. She seriously considers her wants
> and needs.*)

IDA. I wanna go to school.

WYNN. Good.
Yeah.
Definitely.
I think you'd do well.

IDA. I wanna get a job I like.
And I think I have to learn more things
before I can work at the places I wanna work.

WYNN. Absolutely.

IDA. I wanna be your equal.

WYNN. For sure.

IDA. Where you gonna take me?

WYNN. Where you wanna go?

IDA. I want a nice place.

Lots of windows.

Lots of light. I want to see the sky.

I want a view. Not just staring into the side of another building.

WYNN. Okay.

IDA. And I want a big refrigerator.

With an icemaker.

WYNN. Crushed, shredded, and cubed.

IDA. And I don't want all this noise all the time.

I want it to be quiet.

WYNN. Done.

Whatever you want, Ida.

=.=

You'll tell your mama?

You're coming to be with me?

IDA. You wanna be there with me?

When I tell her?

I want you there.

She won't act too crazy if you're there smiling at her.

WYNN. Yeah. Okay. I will.

(They kiss.)

No more Pigeon.

IDA. No more.

Day

(Two crates full of junk, a pile of dresses, a footstool, a bathroom sink, a yellow rug, and a bicycle wheel with the u-lock still attached surround **KLASS**.*)*

(The notebook straddles the back of the bench. The Destiny's Child cover hangs horizontal. The trio of smiling faces gleam at the audience.)

*(***KLASS*** stands next to the notebook. His coat is on the ground among the other things. He's wearing a brown T-shirt with unreadable markings on it. Looks as if someone slashed it with a black Sharpie. On the other side of* **KLASS** *is a pile of T-shirts. An assortment of sizes and colors.)*

*(***KLASS*** has rearranged his possessions in the curved shape of a bustling crowd. He addresses the objects around him as if he's addressing an eager and devout congregation.)*

(Side note: **KLASS** *evokes a performance style similar to that of Robert Preston's "Trouble" from* The Music Man, *1962. He also taps into a Baptist minister style à la Reverend B.W. Smith. If a middle ground can be found between these two, that'd be so, so cool.)*

KLASS. You may not be
fully aware of the times we're livin' in.

The times that they don't print in our papers or splash across our screens or pump through our radios.

I suggest you might not be aware because I see you. I watch you.

I see you holding on to what little sanity and security you have left,

squeezing it so tight that the color is leaving your fingers, draining from your hands.

The squeezing is causing your muscles to ache. Jaws to clench.

And you think that pain is a sign of sanity?

Security?

It's not, my friends.

It's not.

=.=

There's a wind blowin' through you.

=.=

A violent gust of truth.

=.=

It starts out as a breeze somewhere in here: *(Points at his heart.)*

and it wakes up all the noise inside of you.

Then that breeze gets in your blood. Travels through every vein. Head to toe.

It gathers enough speed to the point where it won't let you sleep at night.

That breeze becomes a gust and that gust won't let you be still. Won't keep your troubles quiet.

You sit on stoops, lean against cars, stand under the moon – restless.

You walk to one end of your neighborhood then back to the other end, go sit back on that same stoop, sit under the sun – restless.

The gust is stirring your soul.

It's pulling up memories from way down deep,

from the cracks and crevices covered with scabs and scars.

We swallow what we think is liquor,

inhale what we think is weed,

inject what we think is freedom.

We alter our state of reality

so we don't have to participate in it.

So we can't be responsible, aware, dependable.

And what happens when we hear a scream?

When we see someone who looks like us, cornered?
Pleading?
Hm?

>(**KLASS** *turns away as if he's ignoring a
>weeping soul.*)

We cross the street.
We turn the music up a little louder.
We drink, smoke, squeeze...
but we still hear it. It never goes away.
The wind, the noise, that somebody pleading...
it's not going away.
And then the next somebody is cornered.

>(**KLASS** *turns away.*)

And then the next one...

>(*He turns away.*)

And then the next – until it's you.
And then you want to know why
no one's coming to save you, to take you to a safe place?

>(*Throughout the rest of his speech,* **KLASS**
>*slowly sheds the "performance." His genuine
>self floats to the surface.*)

I know it's scary.
It's terrifying when you hear about
Thick Necks taking dudes out,
and
and you hear about drug heads
snatching bags,
and you see people walkin' the streets, talking crazy.
All you wanna do is turn away.
But, but we shouldn't do that anymore.

>(**KLASS** *gestures to the pile of T-shirts next to
>him.*)

I made these protest T-shirts.

You can pick whatever you want.
Take whichever you want.
Each one of them says different things.
I wrote different things on each one.

> (**KLASS** *grabs a T-shirt from the pile. Holds it
> up. The message is unreadable.*)

This one says:
Hi, my name is Klass.
I live on a bench
in the David L. Hynn projects.
Say "good morning" when you pass by.
I won't hurt you.

> (*He tosses that shirt out into the crowd of
> objects.*)

> (*He picks up another one from the pile.
> Displays it. The message is unreadable.*)

And this one says:
I used to sleep in a shelter in another city
far, far from here.

> (*He tosses it. Grabs another one.*)

And this one says:
My daddy used to be the super here.
His name was Paul.
He went to people's apartments and fixed things.
He was very nice.

> (*Toss. Reads from another shirt.*)

My daddy taught me how to change
the chain on my bike.
I don't know if I ever loved him.
I just know he fixed things that
were broken
and then I could go play outside.

> (*Toss. Another.*)

My moms wanted me to have siblings: a brother and a sister.

My daddy wanted to name my baby brother Taylor and my baby sister Grace.

My dad is the one who named me Klass with a "K."

(Toss. Another.)

My name isn't Pigeon.

(He flips the T-shirt over to the backside.)

You think you can call me whatever you want but you can't. You don't know me.

(Toss. He picks up another shirt.)

I used to live with my family in building one.

*(**KLASS** points in the direction of building one.)*

I got pulled out when I was a kid.

(Toss. Another shirt.)

This is a fire.

And this... *(He points to a spot on the shirt.)* is my folks in the fire.

*(**KLASS** turns the shirt over to the back.)*

These are the hands that pulled me out.

(He drops the shirt on the ground. Letting it fall wherever. He's lost interest in the crowd. He travels back into his memories.)

(He picks up another shirt, but doesn't bother displaying it. From this point on he addresses the shirts as if he's going through a photo album.)

This is the room they put me in at the hospital.

I was a kid. I was eight.

(Drop. Another shirt.)

A social worker told me what happened to my folks.

She hugged me. I remember the side of my face pressed against her chest.

That was the night the system got a hold of me and didn't let go 'til I was eighteen.

(Drop. Another shirt.)

This is the dude who started the fire.

He lived in the apartment below ours.

He was a few years older than me.

He used to kick my ass every day.

(Another shirt.)

This is the foster building I lived in for ten years.

The day I got out I found that dude

who started the fire and slammed him in the face with a brick.

(Flips the shirt to the backside.)

Here's a picture of that brick.

*(**KLASS** drops that shirt. He looks down at the one he's wearing.)*

And this one is me

in the future

fixing the chain on my daughter's bike.

(He stretches to catch a glimpse of the back.)

This is me and her mother watching our daughter ride around.

*(**KLASS** waves at his future.)*

All these shirts are free.

Take however many you want.

(He steps down from the bench. Sits. He looks at the notebook.)

Justice for our streets.

Justice means peace.

Justice for our...streets.

Justice means...

Evening

(**KLASS** *is asleep. The notebook rests in his lap.*)

(**IDA** *enters. Stops at the edge. Looks at* **KLASS**.)

(*She crosses to the other side, then exits.*)

(*Several moments pass.*)

(**IDA** *enters and goes over to* **KLASS**. *She looks at the notebook on his lap.*)

(*She ever so slowly reaches and grabs the notebook, then scurries away on her tiptoes.*)

Night

(Hours later.)

*(**KLASS** wakes with a jump. Reaches for the notebook. It's gone.)*

(He looks around. Nothing.)

(Did he put it back under the coat? No.)

(Is he sitting on it? No.)

(Where is it?)

(He looks under the rug. Pulls out one crate, digs through it, then the other. Pulls out the dresses from the bathroom sink. Shakes out each one. Nothing.)

*(**WYNN** enters.)*

*(**KLASS** spots him.)*

KLASS. Did you steal my stuff?

WYNN. What?

KLASS. Did you steal my stuff?

WYNN. Man, don't nobody want that junk.

> *(**WYNN** keeps walking, **KLASS** leaps into his path. **WYNN** steps back, ready to defend himself.)*

KLASS. I had my notebook when I fell asleep and now it's gone.

WYNN. That ain't got shit to do with me.

KLASS. Did you take it?

WYNN. Look, if you wanna throw down let's do it. None of this talkin' shit.

KLASS. Did you take it!

WYNN. Oh, you wanna yell at a brotha? Crazy mutha–

> *(**WYNN** shoves **KLASS**.)*
>
> *(**KLASS** shoves **WYNN** back.)*

(The duel ensues. They lock horns. The bout builds and builds until **KLASS** *pins* **WYNN** *behind the bench.* **KLASS** *grabs hold of his arm and bends it back until there's a popping sound.)*

WYNN. Ahhhh! Fuck!!

The Following Morning

> (**KLASS** *sleeps on the ground. The dresses cover him like a blanket.*)
>
> (**IDA** *enters and throws the notebook at him.*)
>
> (**KLASS** *snaps awake.*)

IDA. I took it.

KLASS. =.=

IDA. I snatched it while you was sleepin'.

> (**KLASS** *picks up the notebook. Flips through it.*)

I tore out my pages.

KLASS. Why'd you steal it?

IDA. 'Cause I don't want you carryin' me in there anymore.
I was on half those pages and I took my half back.

KLASS. It's my notebook. You just can't go around stealing people's stuff.

IDA. I gave it back, didn't I?
Wynn is bringing his boys to come beat your ass.
You broke his arm.
He works with his hands.
He's losing money 'cause of you.
Is that shit *(Re: the notebook.)* that important to you?
That shit worth taking away somebody's livelihood?

KLASS. Your livelihood, too.

IDA. What?

KLASS. I break his arm; I break your ATM.

IDA. Half the time I'm with you, you don't say shit.
And when you do speak you end up tryin' to talk shit about me?

KLASS. Don't matter if you rip those pages out.
It don't matter.
Doesn't matter, Ida Peters.
Ida Peters.

Ida Peters Ida Peters Ida...

> (**KLASS** *tosses the notebook to the side. He doesn't need it.*)
>
> (*He recites her life as if it's an old Negro chant.*)

Your name is Ida Peters.

You're eighteen years old.

It don't matter if you take those pages from me...

Born and raised in the David L. Hynn housing projects.

No brothers.

No sisters.

Your mama's living on disability checks.

IDA. =.=

KLASS. Your father's been living on the other side of the city all your life.

But you only talked to him three times.

Saw him once.

You have a picture of him from when he was eighteen.

You only know what he looks like when he was your age.

You wouldn't know him if you saw him today. Right now.

You claim you would.

But you know you wouldn't.

You feel like my eyes hold you just like the eyes in your daddy's picture.

IDA. =.=

> (**KLASS** *looks at* **IDA.**)
>
> (*She returns his stone-cold gaze.*)

KLASS. Ida Peters.

I don't need those pages...don't matter if you take 'em from me –

IDA. Klass Washington.

Twenty-five years old.

No brothers.

No sisters.

No mother.

No father.

You're still too scared to fall asleep inside four walls, under a ceiling.

Still too scared if sirens wake you up.

Still need to have a can of grape soda every day because it's the last sweet thing your mama gave you.

You don't consider yourself a real man because you never got the chance to leave home.

Your home left you.

(**KLASS** *gets on his knees.*)

Klass Washington.

I don't need those pages either.

(**IDA** *looks at* **KLASS**.)

(*He returns her stone-cold gaze.*)

KLASS. You want to work behind a desk.

Answering phones for Young White Man Esquire.

You want to wear pretty cotton skirts with the complementary blouses

that makes Young White Man Esquire smile. Readjust his junk.

And maybe...the afternoon before you leave early for Christmas holiday,

you'll let Esquire touch your cheek, (**KLASS** *gestures a grip on* **IDA**'s *ass.*) squeeze your cheek. Bite. Hard.

IDA. You still have the bite marks on your shoulders.

(**IDA** *falls to her knees.*)

Two scars on the left. Three on the right.

One of them was a biter. And if he couldn't bite you there because of the scabs,

he'd chew on the back of you. He'd chew on your hair.

You shaved it off, he'd bite your scalp.

You stopped deciding what was worse: him topping you or the skin breaking on the back of your head. Him drinking your blood.

KLASS. You hear your mama strugglin' to open a drawer or pick up a cup,

but you don't move.

You let her struggle because she's getting what she deserves.

Everything is her fault.

IDA. You were the smallest in that foster home.

And the smallest one gets busted by the bigger ones.

KLASS. You want her to suffer...

IDA. The light-skinned one sits up first...

KLASS. Never no money for nothing.

Only enough for her medication, for her nurse...

No cell phone for you, no new kicks, no new clothes.

IDA. And then he wakes up the one with the crooked teeth...

Then the oldest one gets up...

KLASS. Sometimes you put stuff out of her reach

'cause you know she'll need it.

She'll struggle to get it.

IDA. They surround your bed.

The oldest one flips you over.

They know you're not asleep even though you try to act like it.

KLASS. *(Imitating Ida's mama.)* "Ida! I-da! I know you hear me!

Ida, I need help in the kitchen!!"

IDA. *(Imitating the boys from the foster home.)* "That's right, man. Don't make a fuckin' sound. Keep your mouth shut while we handle this shit right here."

> *(They reach out with one hand and grab each other by the neck at the same time.)*

> *(They squeeze. They strain to breathe but hold on. They look at each other.)*

(The neighborhood bustles. Hip-hop bumps in the distance.)

*(**KLASS** lets go, falls back. **IDA** lets go, falls on top of him.)*

(They roll. He's on top of her. She pushes him away, pulls him in.)

(They roll. She's on top of him. She gets up. He grabs her, pulls her down.)

(She struggles. She surrenders. She pushes. She pulls. He pulls. He struggles. He licks.)

(He surrenders. She bites. He scratches. She grunts. She gasps. He whimpers. He inhales. He releases. She pulls. She wails.)

(They hold. Tears. They hold. Gasp. They hold.)

*(**KLASS** rolls away from her.)*

*(**IDA** stares up at the sky, chasing breath.)*

*(**KLASS** stares up at the sky, chasing breath.)*

*(**IDA** slowly rises to her feet. Without a word or a glance, she walks away.)*

*(**KLASS** watches the sky.)*

Day

(Two crates full of junk, a pile of dresses, a footstool, a pile of T-shirts, a bathroom sink, a yellow rug, a bicycle wheel with a u-lock still attached.)

(No **KLASS.***)*

Night

(Two crates full of junk, a pile of dresses, a footstool, a pile of T-shirts, a bathroom sink, a yellow rug, a bicycle wheel with a u-lock still attached, a microwave, and a box fan.)

(Three cans of soup sit on the bench.)

(The dresses are stuffed into the microwave.)

(The T-shirts are draped across the other bench.)

(No **KLASS***.)*

*(***IDA** *enters, carrying two plastic bags full of groceries. She crosses, exits.)*

Day

(The notebook is shredded; pieces of it blow in the wind.)

(The sink is gone.)

(The lamp is back, tipped over, leaning across a bench.)

(Empty soup cans lay about.)

(No **KLASS.***)*

Evening

(One of the benches is destroyed. The slats are gone. The rusted metal frame remains.)

*(No **KLASS**.)*

*(**WYNN** enters, pulling a big suitcase. His arm in a cast. He crosses, exits.)*

*(**IDA** enters, carrying a box. She crosses, exits.)*

*(**WYNN** enters, crosses, exits.)*

*(**KLASS** enters, wearing his coat. The hood is pulled up, casting a shadow across his face. He carries a colander and a handful of straws.)*

(He sits.)

*(**IDA** enters.)*

*(She sees **KLASS**, keeps her head down.)*

*(**KLASS** ignores her.)*

*(**IDA** crosses. Exits.)*

*(**KLASS** polishes the colander.)*

*(**WYNN** enters, pulling another large suitcase. He redirects his path so that he walks in front of **KLASS**. He purposely and aggressively kicks Klass' things as he crosses.)*

*(**KLASS** ignores him.)*

(He polishes his colander.)

WYNN. *(Mumbles.)* Dumb ass, punk.

*(**WYNN** exits.)*

*(**KLASS** puts the colander down. Fishes for the salt & pepper shakers. He polishes them.)*

*(**IDA** enters, carrying too much.)*

(She drops a few things.)

*(**KLASS** ignores her.)*

(**IDA** *puts everything down and reorganizes her load.*)

(*She picks it all up again, crosses, and exits.*)

(**KLASS** *stops polishing, turns his head to watch her. He pulls down his hood, revealing a bruised and swollen face.*)

Night

*(***KLASS** *is asleep.)*

(He wakes up with a jump. He bats at the back of his head, his neck.)

KLASS. *(Terrorized.)* Get away from me!
Get away from me...

(He falls off the bench, scoots away from his invisible predator, throwing objects in its path.)

*(***KLASS** *musters up the courage to stand up for himself. He scrambles to his feet.)*

Come on!
Come on!
Let's do this for real.
Come on, muthafucka!

(He wrestles with the air. Falls to the ground. Wiggles out of his coat. Springs back to his feet.)

Ha! Yeah, you thought you had me!
You ain't got shit!

(Another razzle-dazzle move, Muhammad Ali-style. **KLASS** *goes in for the attack.)*

Blam!
Blam!
Blam!
Blam!
Try and breathe after that, punk bitch!

(Victorious, winded, **KLASS** *falls to the ground.)*

(Without warning, a police light lands on him. **KLASS** *is wild-eyed, shields his face from the light.)*

(A voice comes from behind the light.)

THICK NECK 1. Hello.

KLASS. =.= *(Breathing.)*

THICK NECK 1. How are you feelin' tonight?

KLASS. =.=

THICK NECK 1. Everything all right?

KLASS. =.=

THICK NECK 1. We got a call about a disturbance.
    Makin' sure everything is all right.

KLASS. =.=

THICK NECK 1. My name is Officer Ryan.
    What's your name?

KLASS. I don't wanna go to jail.

THICK NECK 1. What's that?

KLASS. =.=

THICK NECK 1. You have some ID I can take a look at?

KLASS. No.

THICK NECK 1. You got somewhere you can go tonight?

KLASS. No.

THICK NECK 1. People tell us you been stayin' here on these
    benches for awhile.

KLASS. =.=

THICK NECK 1. Where are you coming from?

KLASS. =.=

THICK NECK 1. What's your name?

KLASS. They call me Pigeon.

THICK NECK 1. Is that your real name?

KLASS. =.=

THICK NECK 1. Well, Pigeon, I'm afraid I can't let you stay
    here tonight.

        (A siren pulls up, shuts off. Another light on
        KLASS.*)*

Tenants called in.

We have to remove you.

KLASS. This is where I live.

THICK NECK 1. We can check around with a few shelters.
See if they have beds tonight.

KLASS. No. No shelters. No beds.
I want to stay here.

THICK NECK 2. It's usually easier to get a bed in the summer
months.

KLASS. What about my stuff?!
I have things that I need to keep with me.
I can't leave any of it. And the shelter won't protect it.
Somebody'll take it.

THICK NECK 1 & 2. Whoa...hey, calm down...

THICK NECK 1. We won't let anyone take your things.
We will need you to calm down.

THICK NECK 2. *(To* **THICK NECK 1.***)* What's his name?

THICK NECK 1. Says it's "Pigeon."

THICK NECK 2. Clever...
Pigeon, we won't let anyone steal your stuff, okay?
But you'll have to calm down.
We're here to help you.

KLASS. I don't need any help.

THICK NECK 1. Well, we disagree.
And the residents in these apartments disagree.

KLASS. =.=

> *(Another siren pulls up. Shuts off. Three
> lights on* **KLASS.***)*

THICK NECK 2. We can take you to get your face fixed.
Looks like somebody got you good.
Who did that to you?

KLASS. Nobody.

THICK NECK 1. Well, you should get that fixed up.
Infections can happen before you know it.

> *(Another motorcycle pulls up. Shuts off. Four
> lights on* **KLASS.***)*

(**THICK NECKS** *talk amongst themselves.* **KLASS** *strains to see past the beams of light.*)

THICK NECK 1. Stinks to high hell.

THICK NECK 3. No track marks.

THICK NECK 1. Well, there's obviously something wrong with him.

THICK NECK 2. Think the ward'll take him?

THICK NECK 3. Maybe.

THICK NECK 1. Hey, Pigeon,

let's take you somewhere safe, all right?

(**KLASS***' eyes grow big and wild as the lights get closer. He screams. Flails. Starts swinging.*)

KLASS. I don't want to leave!

I can't leave.

Don't take me anywhere!

I didn't do anything!

I didn't do anything!

(*Police lights out. Sounds of a scuffle.*)

(*A zap.*)

(**KLASS** *falls to the ground. He moans.*)

Day

(Neighborhood sounds.)

*(No **KLASS**.)*

(All of his things are gone.)

(The two benches are gone.)

*(**IDA** enters, upset. **WYNN** follows. The cast on his arm is gone.)*

WYNN. Ida, slow down.

IDA. Ugh, she gets on my last nerve, Wynn.

Where she comin' from sayin' all that shit to me?

To my face!

And expect me to sit there and take it?

WYNN. She ain't right, Ida.

You know that. I know that.

IDA. I don't care.

She still my mama.

She need to act like she got some respect for me.

I'm a married woman.

I'm in school.

I know things.

Tellin' me I don't know shit about life.

She ain't never really lived hers.

How she gonna judge what I do with mine?

WYNN. She's just sad.

Sad you left.

Sad you been gone.

IDA. Why are you stickin' up for her?

WYNN. I'm not stickin' up for her.

IDA. Yes, you are.

Don't forget she was bustin' on you, too.

Calling you weak.

Said you foolish for putting up with me.

WYNN. She don't know what she's talkin' 'bout.
She don't know what she's sayin'.

IDA. She says it like she does.

WYNN. She don't.
Your mama sits up in that apartment all day
watching TV, drinking Diet Coke.
She ain't aware of half the shit she say.
She just talk to be talking.

IDA. You can let it roll easy,
because she's not your mother.

=.=

=.=

I don't wanna come back here again.

WYNN. You don't mean that.

IDA. I do.

WYNN. Ida, you don't.

IDA. This is the last time I wanna walk anywhere near here.
I don't wanna see her again.
Don't wanna walk across this courtyard.
Don't wanna hear all this bullshit noise ever again.

WYNN. You gonna miss it. Miss her.

IDA. No. No I won't.
And don't make it seem like I'm fickle.

WYNN. Take it easy, gurl.
Don't flip out on me, too.

IDA. =.=

=.=

I bring up one thing about seeing my father and she...

(**WYNN** *hugs her.* **IDA** *relaxes.*)

Thank you for coming with me.

WYNN. You're welcome, my baby.

IDA. Thank you for anchoring me.

WYNN. Because I love you, Ida.

IDA. Thank you for takin' care of me.

WYNN. I love you, Ida.

IDA. You saved me.

WYNN. Because I love you.

IDA. I was kickin', screamin', wailing for help
and
you saved me.

> (**IDA** *kisses* **WYNN**.)

Will you take me home?

WYNN. I'll take you wherever you want to go.

> (*They exit, holding hands.*)
>
> (*Distorted hip-hop music bumps in the distance.*)

End of Play

CPSIA information can be obtained
at www.ICGtesting.com
Printed in the USA
BVHW040220170821
614603BV00014B/681